This Bing book belongs to:

.. ..

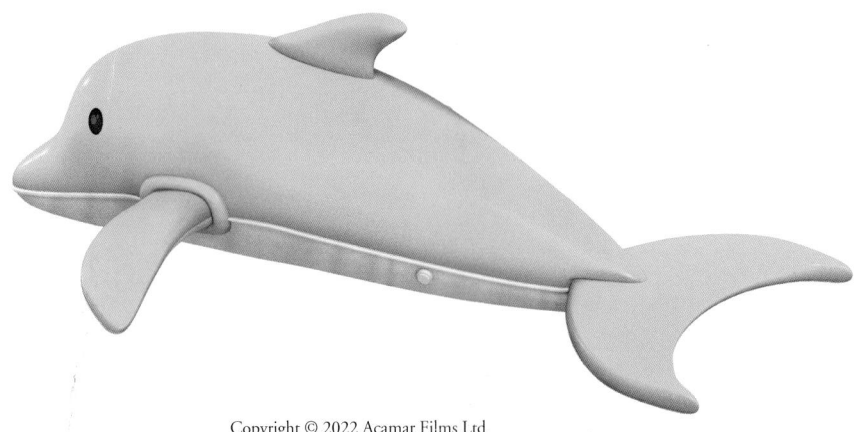

The *Bing* television series is created by Acamar Films and Brown Bag Films
and adapted from the original books by Ted Dewan.

Bing's Bus Ride is based on the original story 'Bus Ride' written by Denise Cassar, Mikael Shields and Claire Jennings. *Bing's Bus Ride*
was first published in the United Kingdom by HarperCollins *Children's Books* in 2022 and was adapted from the original story by Rebecca Gerlings.

HarperCollins *Children's Books* is a division of HarperCollins*Publishers* Ltd
1 London Bridge Street, London SE1 9GF

www.harpercollins.co.uk

HarperCollins*Publishers*
1st Floor, Watermarque Building, Ringsend Road, Dublin 4, Ireland

1 3 5 7 9 10 8 6 4 2

ISBN: 978-0-00-849773-6

Printed in the UK by Pureprint a CarbonNeutral® company

MIX
Paper from
responsible sources
FSC
www.fsc.org
FSC® C007454

This book is produced from independently certified FSC™ paper
to ensure responsible forest management.

For more information visit: www.harpercollins.co.uk/green

Bing

Bing's Bus Ride

HarperCollins *Children's Books*

Round the corner, not far away,
Bing is going on **the bus** today.

"We're going to the SEASIDE!" says Bing.

"Seaside! Seaside!" shouts Pando.

"Oh, can you blow up Mr Dolphin, Flop?" asks Bing.

"When we get to the seaside, Bing," Flop replies. "If we blow him up now he'll be too big to take on the bus!"

Flop puts a few last things into Wheelie and they are ready to go.

"Okay, let's **go, go, go, go, gooo!"** everyone
shouts excitedly as they make their way to the bus stop.
"Seaside! Seaside!"

"When's the bus coming, Flop?" asks Bing.

Flop checks his phone.
"Hmmm, it'll be here soon, Bing," he replies.

"Let's see who can spot the bus first," says Padget.

"Oooh! I can see one, I can see one!" shouts Pando.

One bus drives past . . . but it's not going to the seaside. Another bus drives past . . . but it's going in the opposite direction.

"It's OK, Bing. There are lots of buses, all going to different places," explains Flop. "Ours is still coming."

"When is it coming?" asks Bing.

"Now! Now!" shouts Pando, as a blue bus pulls into the bus stop.

Bing and Pando wait for some
passengers to get off, then they jump aboard.

"We're going to the seaside!" they shout together.

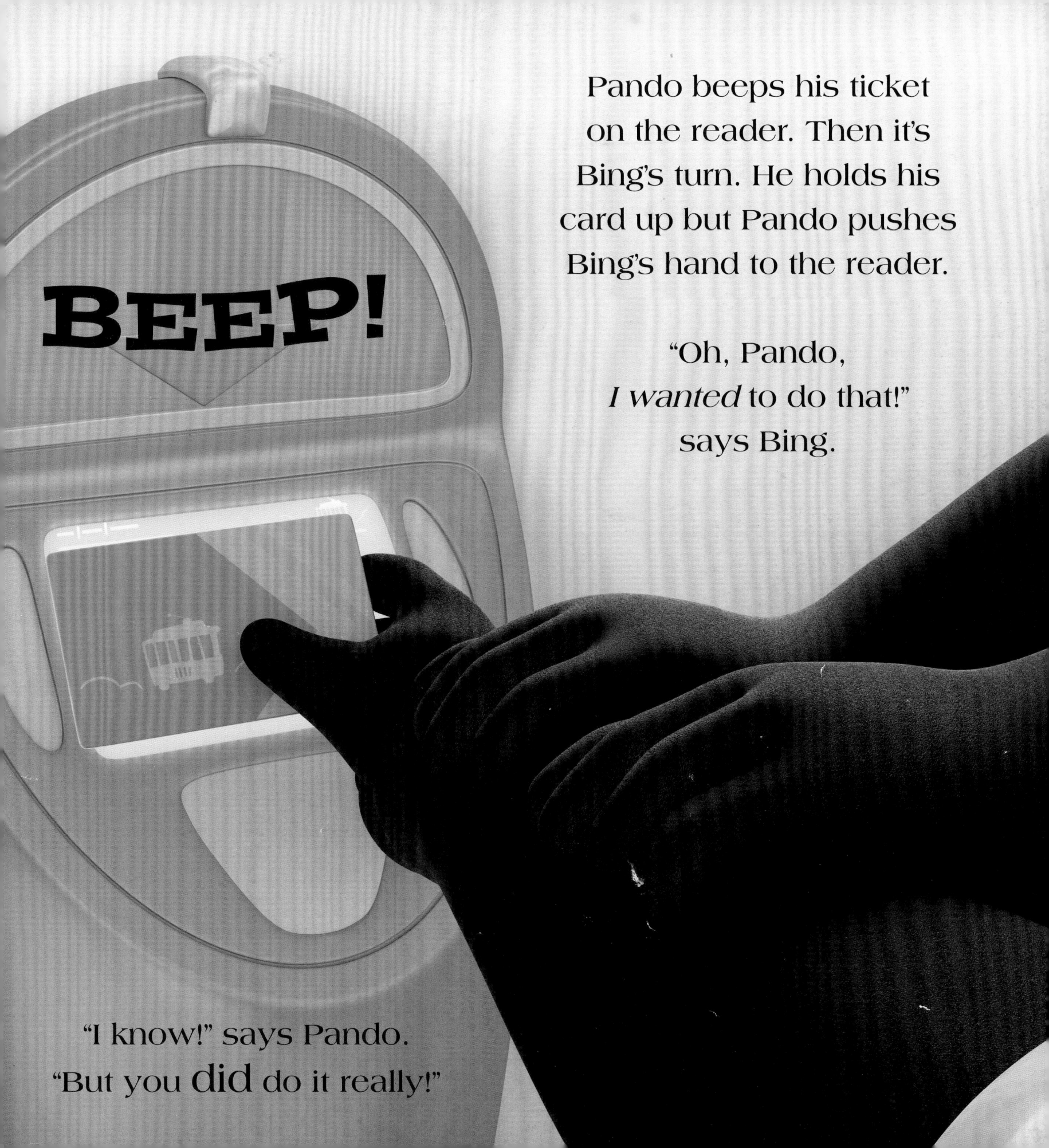

BEEP!

Pando beeps his ticket on the reader. Then it's Bing's turn. He holds his card up but Pando pushes Bing's hand to the reader.

"Oh, Pando, *I wanted* to do that!" says Bing.

"I know!" says Pando. "But you **did** do it really!"

Now it's time to find a seat . . . but Pando pushes
in front of Bing and sits down by the window.

"Pando, *I wanted* to sit by the window!" says Bing.

"Me too! My turn first!" smiles Pando,
as Bing sits down next to him.

"Well," says Flop, "you can take
it in turns to have the window seat."

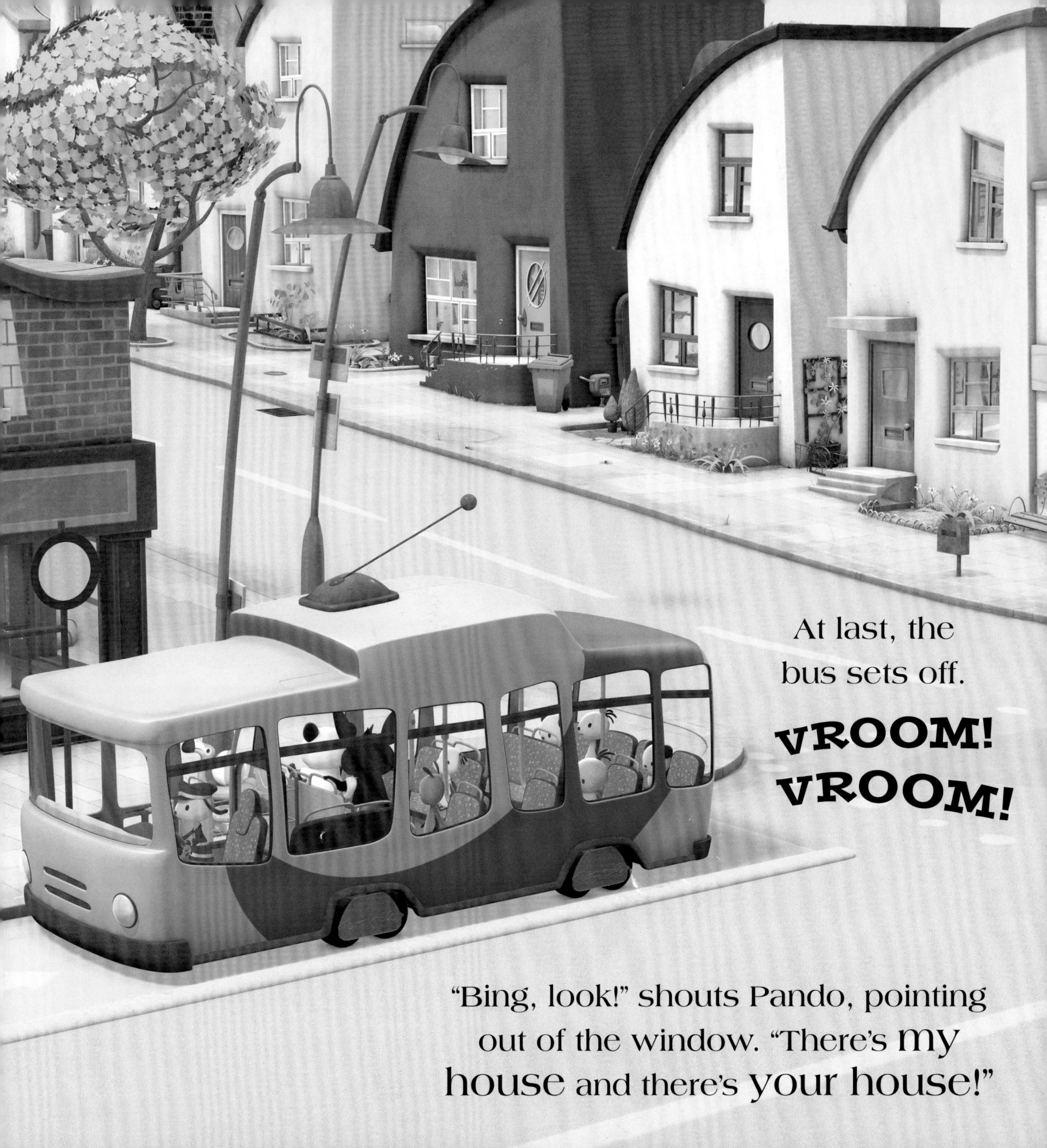

At last, the bus sets off.

VROOM! VROOM!

"Bing, look!" shouts Pando, pointing out of the window. "There's my house and there's your house!"

"Vroom vroom, bus!
Bye-bye, house!" sings Flop.

Bing, Pando and Padget join in.
"Vroom vroom, bus! Bye-bye, house!"

"There's Arlo!"
shouts Bing, peering
out of the window.

"Vroom vroom,
bus! Bye-bye, Arlo!"
everyone sings.

"There's the library!" shouts Pando.

"Vroom vroom, bus! Bye-bye, library!"
everyone sings.

Then suddenly the bus comes to a stop . . .

"Why have we stopped, Flop?" Bing asks.

"I'm not sure," Flop replies.

"Maybe some more people are getting on?" suggests Pando.
But Padget explains that this isn't a bus stop.

The bus driver turns round to makes an announcement over the speaker.

"Good afternoon, passengers," she says. "I need to call the garage because the electric motor has broken."

"I'm very sorry to have to tell you . . ." the bus driver continues, "I can't take you to the seaside today."

"OH NO!" gasp Bing and Pando.

Bing asks Flop if they can still go on the bus to the seaside, but Flop explains, "I'm afraid this is the last seaside bus today, and it's broken down."

"Oh no! But . . . I wanted to ride on the bus, Flop.
And do swimming. And I wanted to sit in the window seat.
And blow up my dolphin," explains Bing.
"And I am disappointed."

"I know, Bing," replies Flop.

Pando offers Bing the window seat.

But there's nothing to see now the bus isn't moving.

All the passengers make their way off the bus.

"Maybe they'll bring a tow truck!" exclaims Pando,
as he and Padget follow them.

Bing and Flop
are the only
passengers left.

"I'm disappointed too,"
says the bus driver.
"It's not very nice when you
want to drive people to the seaside but your bus breaks down."

Just then, she has an idea . . .

"Would you like
to sit in the driver's
seat?" asks the
bus driver.

"Can I, Flop?"
asks Bing.

"Of course,"
Flop replies.

Bing climbs into
the driver's seat.
"Look, Flop!
Vroom vroom!"

"Well, that does
look like fun!"
laughs Flop.

The bus driver lets Bing try her special card – and the horn!

BEEP! BEEP!

"Pando! Look! I'm driving the bus!"
says Bing as Pando climbs on board again.
"Tap the special card on the screen, please."

"You need some passengers, Bing," says Flop. He unpacks **Mr Dolphin** and blows him up. "Here we are!"

"Hello, Mr Dolphin!" Bing calls. "Thank you, Flop!"

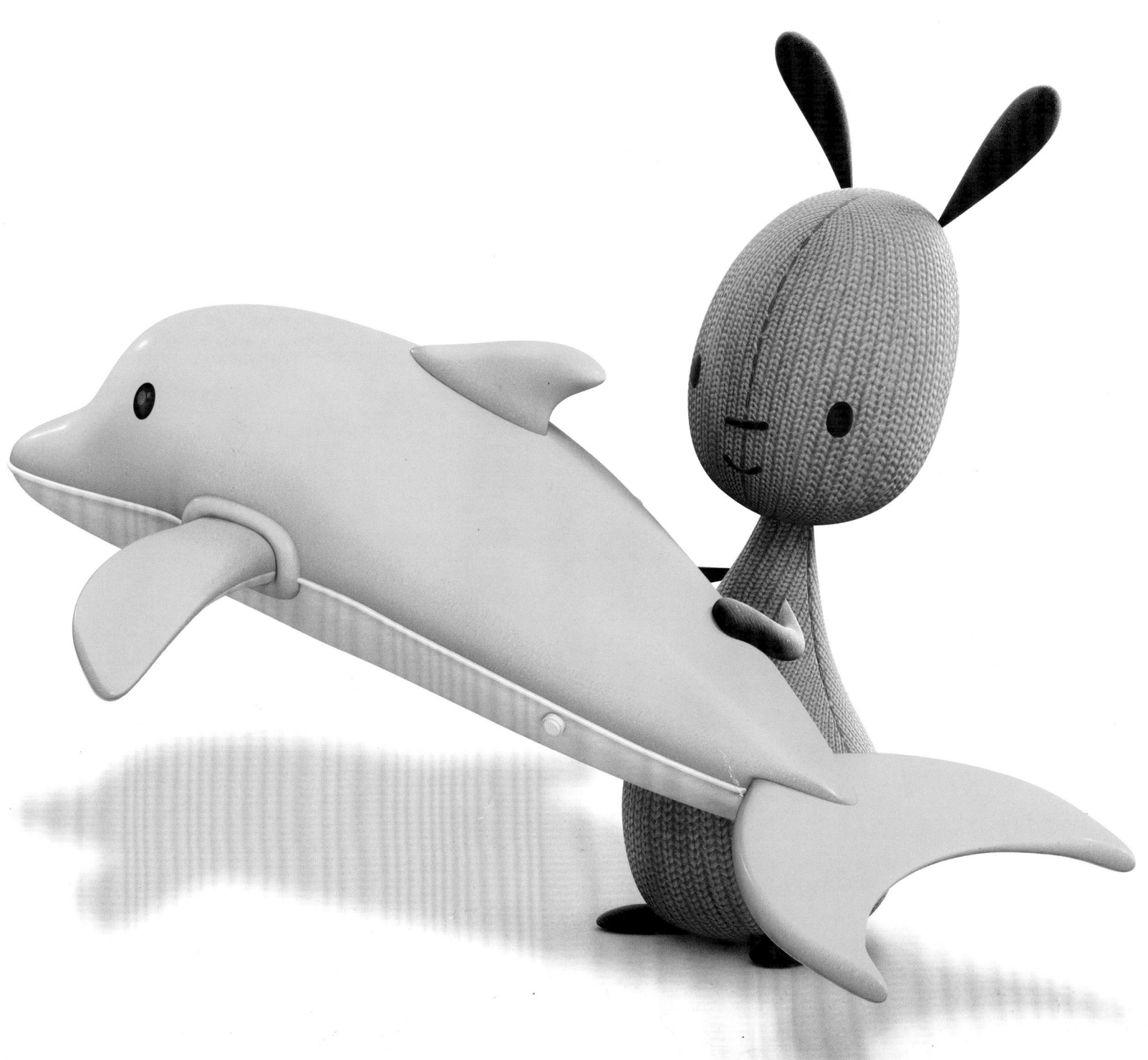

Pando, Flop, Padget, Mr Dolphin and the bus driver all take their seats. "Here we go! Now we're going past the park," announces Bing.

"Vroom vroom, bus! Bye-bye, park!" everyone sings.

Then, finally, Bing pretends to drive past Padget's shop . . .

"Vroom vroom, bus! Bye-bye, shop!" they all sing happily together.

Going on the bus . . . it's a Bing thing!